A Note to Parents

Welcome to REAL KIDS READERS, a series of phonics-based books for children who are beginning to read. In the classroom, educators use phonics to teach children how to sound out unfamiliar words, providing a firm foundation for reading skills. At home, you can use REAL KIDS READERS to reinforce and build on that foundation, because the books follow the same basic phonic guidelines that children learn in school.

Of course the best way to help your child become a good reader is to make the experience fun—and REAL KIDS READERS do that, too. With their realistic story lines and lively characters, the books engage children's imaginations. With their clean design and sparkling photographs, they provide picture clues that help new readers decipher the text. The combination is sure to entertain young children and make them truly want to read.

REAL KIDS READERS have been developed at three distinct levels to make it easy for children to read at their own pace.

- LEVEL 1 is for children who are just beginning to read.
- LEVEL 2 is for children who can read with help.
- LEVEL 3 is for children who can read on their own.

A controlled vocabulary provides the framework at each level. Repetition, rhyme, and humor help increase word skills. Because children can understand the words and follow the stories, they quickly develop confidence. They go back to each book again and again, increasing their proficiency and sense of accomplishment, until they're ready to move on to the next level. The result is a rich and rewarding experience that will help them develop a lifelong love of reading.

To Anne Marie Baumann,
Maryann Pasqualone, Ellen Kenny Pollice, and
Cheryl Tizio (aka Aunt Tizio), for all of your
support and laughter throughout the years
—L. V. T.

Special thanks to Hanna Andersson, Portland, OR,
for providing clothing.

Produced by DWAI / Seventeenth Street Productions, Inc.
Reading Specialist: Virginia Grant Clammer

Library of Congress Cataloging-in-Publication Data

Tidd, Louise.
    Did you hear about Jake? / Louise Vitellaro Tidd ; photographs by Dorothy Handelman.
        p.   cm. — (Real kids readers. Level 2)
    Summary: Jake tells his friend Hank that he's learning to bake, but Hank misunderstands
and begins a chain of misinformation that spreads throughout school.
    ISBN 0-7613-2058-X (lib. bdg.). — ISBN 0-7613-2083-0 (pbk.)
    [1. Communication—Fiction. 2. Schools—Fiction.] I. Handelman, Dorothy, ill.
II. Title. III. Series.
PZ7.T4345Di   1999
[E]—dc21   98-33787
                                                                        CIP
                                                                        AC

pbk: 10 9 8 7 6 5 4 3 2
lib: 10 9 8 7 6 5 4 3 2

Did You Hear About Jake?

By **Louise Vitellaro Tidd**

Photographs by **Dorothy Handelman**

M

The Millbrook Press

Brookfield, Connecticut

Jake was in the kitchen.
He was using the mixer.
The phone rang.
It was his friend Hank.
"Hi," said Hank. "What's new?"
"I can't talk now," said Jake.
"I'm learning to bake."

The mixer was noisy.
"What?" said Hank.
"I can't hear you very well."
But it was too late.
Jake had hung up the phone.

The next day at school,
Hank saw his friend Fran.
He stopped to tell her Jake's news.
"Hi, Fran," he said.

"You know our friend Jake?
He sat on a cake."

The classroom was noisy.
"What?" said Fran.
"I didn't hear you very well."
But it was too late.
Hank had gone on to his desk.

Later, the class went to gym.
Fran was on a team with Fred.
"Did you hear the news?" she said.

"It's all about Jake.
He fell in the lake."

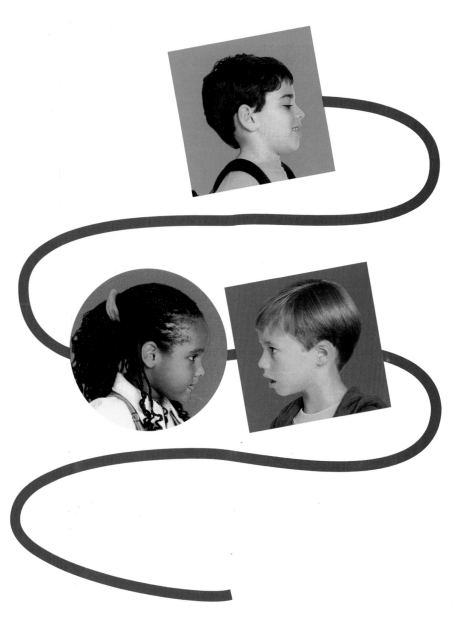

The gym was noisy.
"What?" said Fred.
"I didn't hear you very well."
But it was too late.
Fran was heading for the basket.

After gym, it was time for lunch.
Fred got in line with Kim.
"I have some funny news," he said.

"Did you know that Jake
has a nose that is fake?"

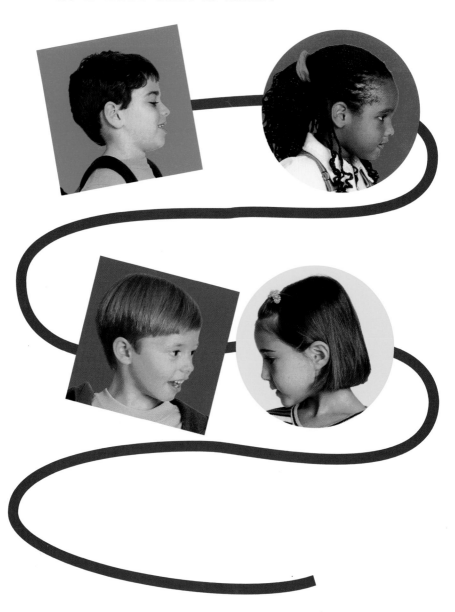

The lunchroom was noisy.
"What?" said Kim.
"I didn't hear you very well."
But it was too late.
Fred had left to sit with friends.

After lunch, Kim went outside.
She played with Kelly.
"Fred told me something funny,"
Kim said to Kelly.

21

"You know that kid Jake?
He was scared by a snake."

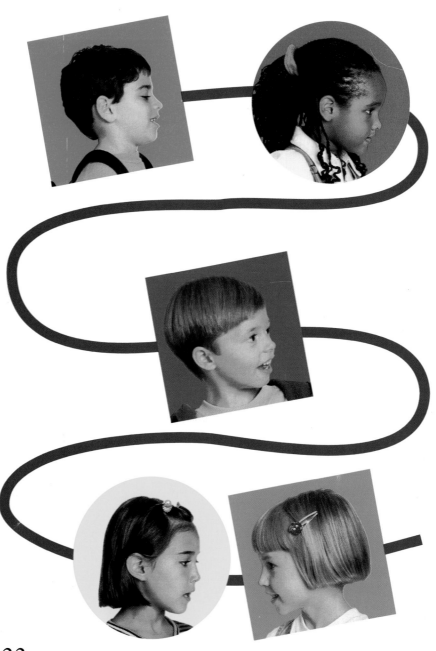

It was noisy outside.
"What?" said Kelly.
"I didn't hear you very well."
But it was too late.
The bell rang,
and Kim ran inside.

When school was over,
Kelly got on the bus with Will.
"Did you hear the news?" she said.

"That sleepy Jake
could not stay awake."

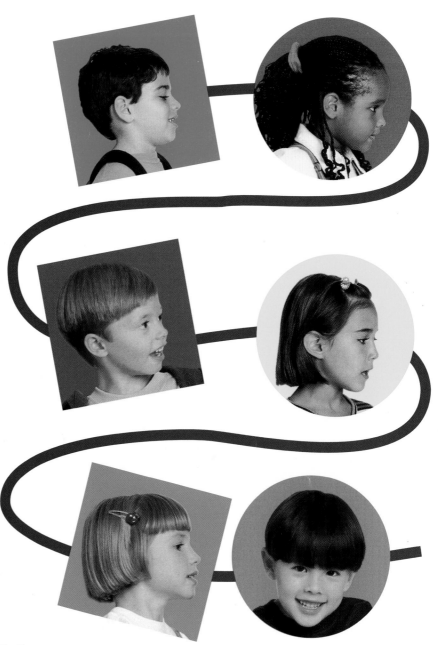

The school bus was noisy.
"What?" said Will.
"I didn't hear you very well."
But it was too late.
Kelly got off the bus.

When Will got home,
he called Hank on the phone.
He told Hank what he had heard.
"That's news to me," said Hank.

Hank went over to Jake's house.
Jake was in the kitchen.
"Hi," said Hank.
"I heard the news, Jake.
You are learning to bake."

"No kidding," said Jake.
"I told you that last night!"

Phonic Guidelines

Use the following guidelines to help your child read the words in *Did You Hear About Jake?*

Short Vowels

When two consonants surround a vowel, the sound of the vowel is usually short. This means you pronounce *a* as in apple, *e* as in egg, *i* as in igloo, *o* as in octopus, and *u* as in umbrella. Short-vowel words in this story include: *bus, but, did, got, had, has, his, kid, Kim, not, ran, sat, sit.*

Short-Vowel Words with Consonant Blends

When two or more different consonants are side by side, they usually blend to make a combined sound. In this story, short-vowel words with consonant blends include: *class, desk, Fran, Fred, Hank, hung, last, left, next, rang, went.*

Double Consonants

When two identical consonants appear side by side, one of them is silent. In this story, double-consonants appear in the short-vowel words *bell, fell, tell, well, will,* and in the *all*-family, the words *all* and *called.*

R-Controlled Vowels

When a vowel is followed by the letter *r*, its sound is changed by the *r*. In this story, words with *r*-controlled vowels include: *for, her.*

Long Vowel and Silent E

If a word has a vowel and ends with an *e*, usually the vowel is long and the *e* is silent. Long vowels are pronounced the same way as their alphabet names. In this story, words with a long vowel and silent *e* include: *bake, cake, fake, home, Jake, lake, late, line, nose, snake, time.*

Double Vowels

When two vowels are side by side, usually the first vowel is long and the second vowel is silent. Double-vowel words in this story include: *day, hear, played, stay, team.*

Diphthongs

Sometimes when two vowels (or a vowel and a consonant) are side by side, they combine to make a diphthong—a sound that is different from long or short vowel sounds. Diphthongs are: *au/aw, ew, oi/oy, ou/ow.* In this story, words with diphthongs include: *drew, how, new, now.*

Consonant Digraphs

Sometimes when two different consonants are side by side, they make a digraph that represents a single new sound. Consonant digraphs are: *ch, sh, th, wh.* In this story, words with digraphs include: *lunch, that, what, when, with.*

Silent Consonants

Sometimes when two different consonants appear side by side, one of them is silent. In this story, words with silent consonants include: *talk, know.*

Sight Words

Sight words are those words that a reader must learn to recognize immediately—by sight—instead of by sounding them out. They occur with high frequency in easy texts. Sight words not included in the above categories are: *a, about, after, are, at, by, could, friend, have, he, hi, I, in, is, it, me, no, off, on, our, over, said, school, she, some, the, to, too, up, very, was, you.*